P9-DJV-428

FROM THE FILMS OF

Harry Potter

HONEYDUKES

A SCRATCH & SNIFF ADVENTURE

ISBN 978-1-338-25395-5

10 9 8 7 6 5 4 3 2 1   18 19 20 21 22

Printed in China   68

First edition, 2018 • Photos ©: 9 bubbles: Isaac Zakar/Shutterstock. • By Daphne Pendergrass and Jenna Ballard • Illustrations by Red Central • Book and cover design by Erin McMahon

DO YOU SMELL THAT?

THE SWEET, BUTTERY SCENT WAFTING THROUGH THE AIR?

SCRATCH & SAVOR

That enchanting aroma is

HONEYDUKES,

the most famous sweet shop featured in the Harry Potter films, located at the heart of bustling Hogsmeade. Honeydukes has confections for every occasion: Looking for a chilly treat on a hot day? There's No Melt Ice Cream! What about something with a more exotic flavor? Check the back for blood-flavored lollipops.

WHATEVER YOU'RE CRAVING,
HONEYDUKES IS SURE TO
HAVE SOMETHING FOR YOU . . .

For the adventurous wizard looking for out-of-the-ordinary tastes, one need look no further than

BERTIE BOTT'S EVERY FLAVOR BEANS.

Sardine

Curry

Grass

Earwax

Cinnamon

Liver

Vomit

Bogey

Sprouts

SCRATCH & SAVOR

Baked Beans

Pepper

Tripe

EVERY FLAVOUR BEANS

BERTIE BOTT'S

"They *mean* every flavor," Harry told Ron during their first ride on the Hogwarts Express.

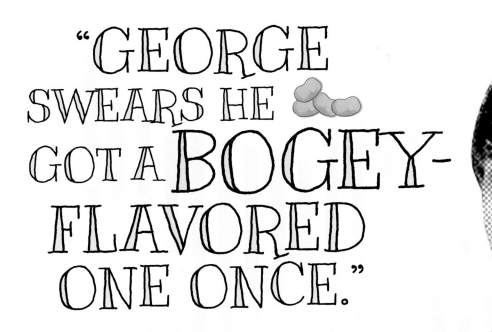

"GEORGE SWEARS HE GOT A BOGEY-FLAVORED ONE ONCE."

George wasn't lying—besides bogey, there's also earwax and vomit, as Albus Dumbledore later attests.

SCRATCH & SAVOR

Harry also picked up his first Chocolate Frog from the Honeydukes Express trolley.

"THESE AREN'T *REAL* FROGS, ARE THEY?"

Harry asked nervously.

"It's just a spell," Ron said. "Besides it's the cards you want. Each pack's got a famous witch or wizard!"

Harry opened up the pack, and the Chocolate Frog leapt from the box and out the train window.

"That's rotten luck," Ron said with a sigh.

"They've only got one good jump in them to begin with."

SCRATCH & SAVOR

LICORICE WANDS

HONEYDUKES

BUT THAT'S NOT ALL—

BUT THAT'S NOT ALL—

the Honeydukes Express trolley is filled with all kinds of confections. Ron was enticed by a

LICORICE WAND

on the trolley in his fourth year, before deciding against it due to the high price.

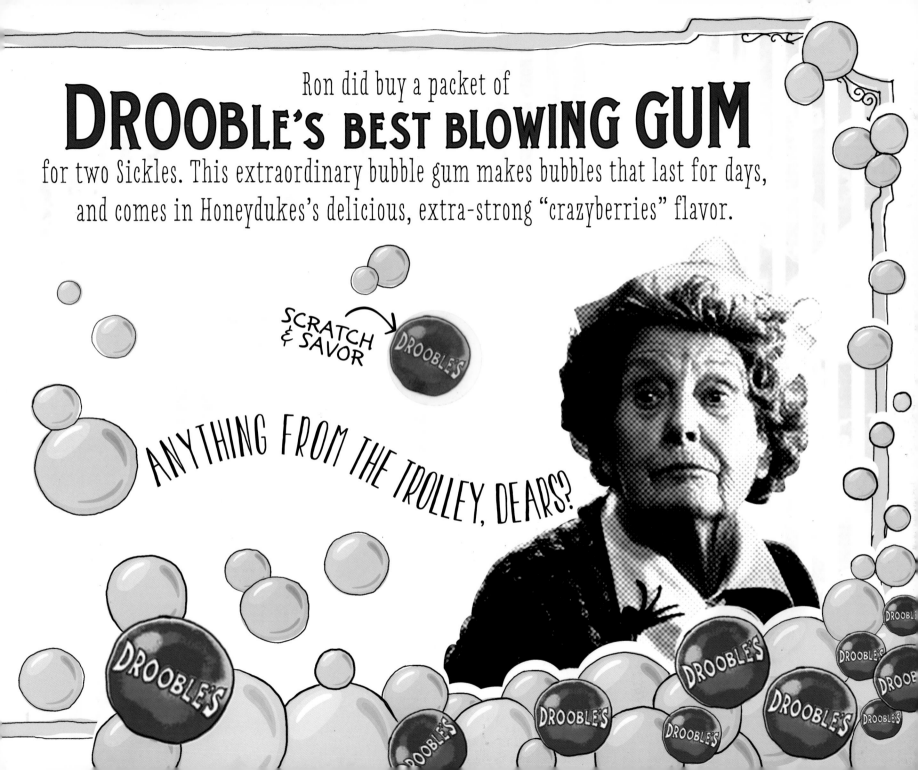

Ron did buy a packet of

DROOBLE'S BEST BLOWING GUM

for two Sickles. This extraordinary bubble gum makes bubbles that last for days, and comes in Honeydukes's delicious, extra-strong "crazyberries" flavor.

SCRATCH & SAVOR

ANYTHING FROM THE TROLLEY, DEARS?

Lots of other fruity sweets can be found on the trolley, including the succulent

FIZZING WHIZBEES.

These chocolatey, fizzy fruits actually buzz in your mouth.

SCRATCH & SAVOR

(Though if a buzzing sweet is what you're after, don't overlook the Fudge Flies!)

Delicious Snack!! Everybody's Favourite!!

QUEENBEE
FIZZING WHIZBEES

made with muggle chocolate and fizzy fruits

BESIDES FRUITY SWEETS,
THE TROLLEY ALSO SELLS SAVORY SNACKS.

Harry developed a crush on Cho Chang after sharing a smile with her at the Honeydukes Express trolley in their fourth year. Cho ordered two Pumpkin Pasties to split with her friends, though it seems Harry would have much rather split them with her. These tiny baked pies have a heavenly pumpkin filling that's irresistible.

SCRATCH & SAVOR

Chocolate and dynamite, a classic combination!

EXPLODING BONBONS

are sure to add a bit of excitement
to a regular day—and perhaps a way to shake off any
sleepiness first thing in the morning.

SCRATCH
& SAVOR

EXPLODING BONBONS

75g   It is a real BOOM!   75g

A treat fit for Fred and George Weasley,

ACID POPS

can double as a practical joke, since it only takes a few licks to burn a hole in one's tongue! Those who fall prey to Acid Pops can be fixed up by a quick trip to Madam Pomfrey—though they'll likely be a bit skeptical of any sweets they're offered in the future.

SCRATCH & SAVOR

HONEYDUKES ACID POPS

Much like Acid Pops, there are more than a few sweets at Honeydukes that one must consume with caution, like

FIERY BLACK PEPPER IMPS

These fiery little treats are one of the hottest sweets around—literally.

During Ron and Hermione's first visit to Hogsmeade, they brought back a stash of Honeydukes sweets, including Pepper Imps, to share with Harry, who wasn't able to go on the trip.

"BE CAREFUL OF THOSE!"
Ron warned, about a second too late.
"THEY'LL MAKE YOU–"

"WHOA!"

SCRATCH & SAVOR

FIERY
BLACK
PEPPER
IMP!

FIERY
BLACK
PEPPE
IMP!

Another dangerous confection that nearly got the better of Harry were

LICORICE SNAPS.

These feisty, black-licorice-flavored nibblers were left in a bowl in Professor Dumbledore's office.

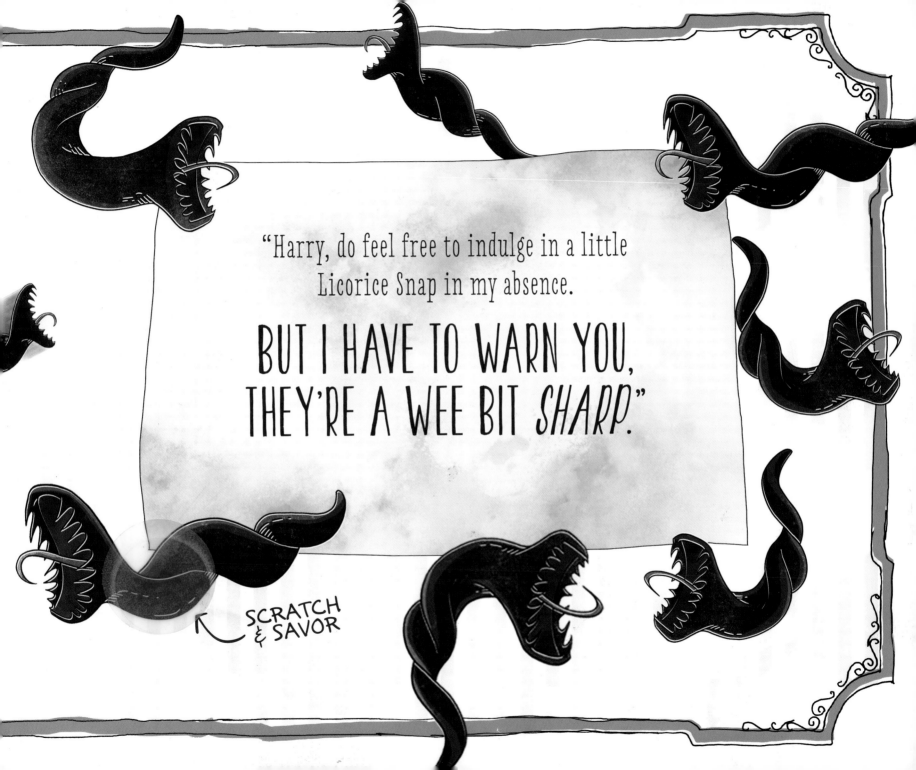

"Harry, do feel free to indulge in a little
Licorice Snap in my absence.

BUT I HAVE TO WARN YOU, THEY'RE A WEE BIT *SHARP*."

SCRATCH
& SAVOR

Dumbledore was very fond of many sweets. His favorite,

SHERBET LEMONS,

were even a password to his office.

SCRATCH & SAVOR

Of course, Dumbledore wasn't the only one interested in unique flavors. After traversing the passageway under the one-eyed witch from Hogwarts to Honeydukes in his Invisibility Cloak, Harry nicked a very unique sweet from Neville Longbottom . . .

A BLOOD-FLAVORED LOLLIPOP.

SCRATCH & SAVOR

Any Hogwarts student who needs a little pick-me-up during an afternoon class knows to break out a

SUGAR QUILL—

perfect for sneaking a taste while pretending to think extra hard about a difficult exam question. Just don't devour the whole thing before the exam is complete!

For witches and wizards who like
their sweets with a bit of wiggle, try

JELLY SLUGS!

These colorful gummy sweets
slide right down your throat. If
only these were the kind of slugs
Ron had conjured with his "Eat
Slugs" curse second year.

SCRATCH
& SAVOR

NO MELT ICE CREAM

SCRATCH & SAVOR

Wizards can savor their sundaes
for as long as they wish with
NO MELT ICE CREAM,
every Muggle's dream on a hot summer day!
This chilled treat is stored right
in the Honeydukes cellars . . . not too far from
the secret passageway back to Hogwarts.

EEEEK!!

Don't be alarmed—this creepy crawly is actually a delicious caramel confection! Anyone who can look past their rather unappetizing appearance will experience the perfect sweet and salty crunch of COCKROACH CLUSTERS.

SCRATCH & SAVOR

But if cockroaches aren't your go-to treat, you can pick up their natural predator, PEPPERMINT TOADS. These bite-sized minty morsels are sure to put a little extra hop in your step.

SCRATCH & SAVOR

Sweet treats, exotic flavors, magic in every bite—there's no doubt that

HONEYDUKES

is one of the best things about the wizarding world.
With endless tastes to try and scents to savor,
we're sure it won't take long for Honeydukes to
come up with another extraordinary sweet that
will have witches and wizards
lined up around the corner.

LICORICE
SNAPS

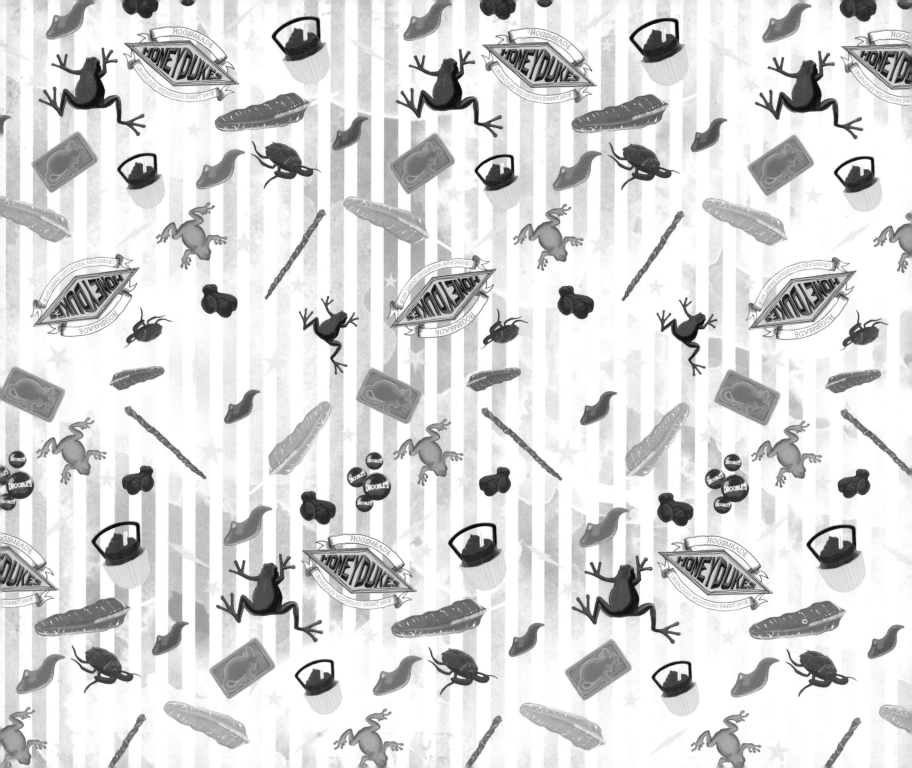